Groundwood Books / House of Anansi Press
groundwoodbooks.com

We gratefully acknowledge for their financial support of our
publishing program the Canada Council for the Arts, the Ontario Arts
Council and the Government of Canada.

Canada Council **Conseil des Arts**
for the Arts **du Canada**

ONTARIO ARTS COUNCIL
CONSEIL DES ARTS DE L'ONTARIO
an Ontario government agency
un organisme du gouvernement de l'Ontario

With the participation of the Government of Canada | **Canadä**
Avec la participation du gouvernement du Canada

Library and Archives Canada Cataloguing in Publication
Title: Where are you, Agnes? / written by Tessa McWatt ;
illustrated by Zuzanna Celej.
Names: McWatt, Tessa, author. | Celej, Zuzanna, illustrator.
Identifiers: Canadiana (print) 20190158859 | Canadiana (ebook)
20190158891 | ISBN 9781773061405 (hardcover) | ISBN 9781773061412
(EPUB) | ISBN 9781773064000 (Kindle)
Subjects: LCSH: Martin, Agnes, 1912-2004—Childhood and
youth—Juvenile fiction.
Classification: LCC PS8575.W37 W44 2020 | DDC jC813/.54—dc23

The illustrations were done in watercolor, collage and
colored pencils on paper.
Design by Michael Solomon
Printed and bound in Malaysia

For Lotte and Otto.

TM

For my mom, Katarzyna.

ZC

Where Are You, Agnes?

WRITTEN BY

Tessa McWatt

ILLUSTRATED BY

Zuzanna Celej

Groundwood Books
House of Anansi Press
Toronto   Berkeley

WHEN Agnes was quite young and her grandfather
was quite old, she fell upon a mystery.
"What do you think?" her grandfather asked.
"It's beautiful," Agnes said.

Then her grandfather did the strangest thing!

"Is it still beautiful?" he asked.

Agnes thought for so long that it seemed she had forgotten the question.

"Yes!" she cried.

Agnes felt something tingling inside.

"Can everyone see that?" she asked.

Her grandfather thought for a long time until it seemed he had forgotten the question.

"I don't exactly know," he said.

Agnes looked from the straight horizon to her grandfather's crooked eyebrows and back again.

And the next day, she picked up her favorite pencil
and began to draw.

Each day, she watched the sky that went on and on
and on in the distance and drew the lines she saw.

Every morning, she watched the birds come and go. And she drew the feeling of the sun and the movement of wings.

She drew the shapes she saw in the wheat, in the tractor tires
and the diamond-shaped lines on the backs of snakes.

She tried to follow the lines to see where they would lead her.

"Where are you, Agnes?" her mother would call to the fields.

But Agnes was following the criss-cross lines in her mind, and she didn't hear.

When her mother asked where she disappeared to while she was drawing, Agnes would say, "I don't exactly know."

One day, her grandfather decided to move the family from
their big house on the prairie to a tiny house in a busy city.

Agnes worried that the birds would never find her.

She searched for snakes, for
rows of wheat and for the straight
horizon, but they had disappeared.

Her brothers and sister liked to ride the carousels and ring the bells at the summer fair.

But Agnes liked to sit beside a tree staring at insects and the patterns they made in the dirt.

"Bugs are creepy," her brothers would say.

"Worms are scary," her sister would say.

But Agnes drew the tiny creatures using her pencil.

As she drew, the feeling of the rainbow would come again . . .

And again . . .

And again . . .

"That doesn't look like a caterpillar," her brother told her one day.

"That's creepy!" her sister said.

And off they went to ring bells and ride carousels.

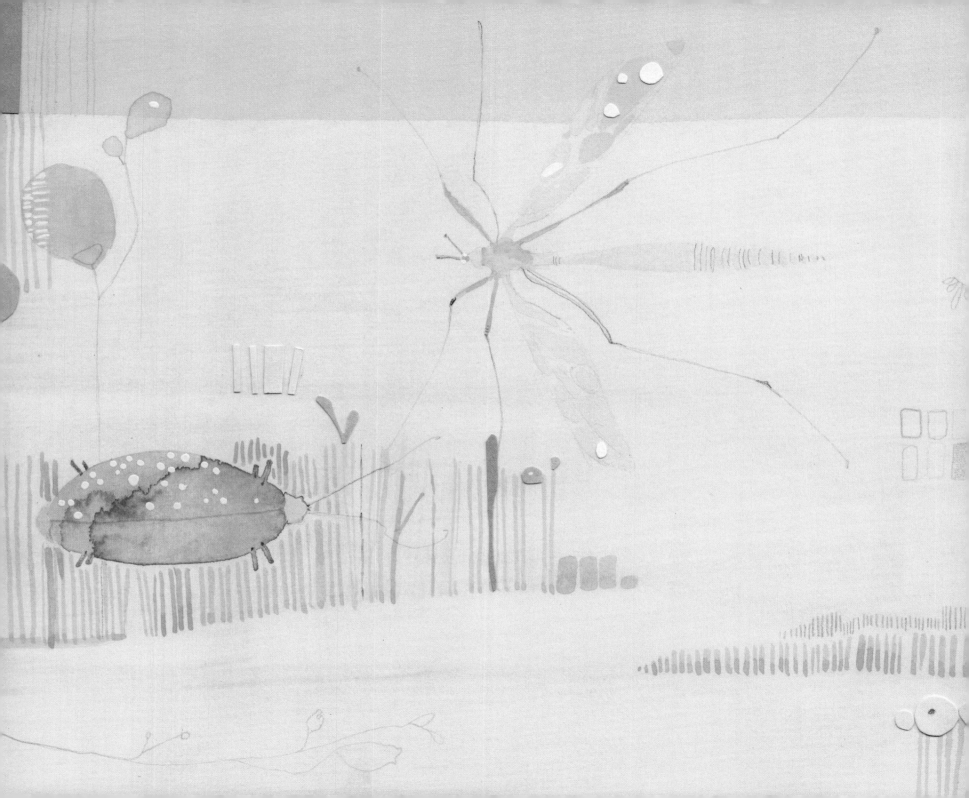

"Where are you, Agnes?" her mother would call
at the end of the day.
   But Agnes was enjoying her drawing so much
that she didn't hear.

At her new school, Agnes wrote curved letters
on the blackboard in chalk.
She loved the feeling of making her name.
But the next morning at school, she felt sad.

Agnes

"Why do things have to disappear?" Agnes asked her grandfather when she got home.

Her grandfather thought for a long time until it seemed he had forgotten the question.

"Let me think more about that one," he said finally.

Her grandfather looked a little pale, so she didn't want to bother him anymore.

It had been a long time since Agnes had felt the rainbow.

She wanted the feeling again, so she went to the park with all her colors.

"That's ugly," her brother said.

So Agnes painted the tree again.

"That's a bit ugly," her sister said.

And she painted again.

And again.

"Where are you, Agnes?" her mother would call,
even when they were in the same room.

Agnes showed her paintings
to her grandfather.
And his eyebrows told her
that she was getting closer.

"But how do I paint a *real* tree?" she asked him as she held on to him tightly, because he seemed so wobbly.

She watched his eyebrows as he thought for so long that it seemed he had forgotten the question.

"The tree won't be there forever," he said finally. "It could be chopped down. It could get rotten and die. But you will remember the tree . . . and see it in other places."

"But how?" she asked.

"Look here," he said, pointing.

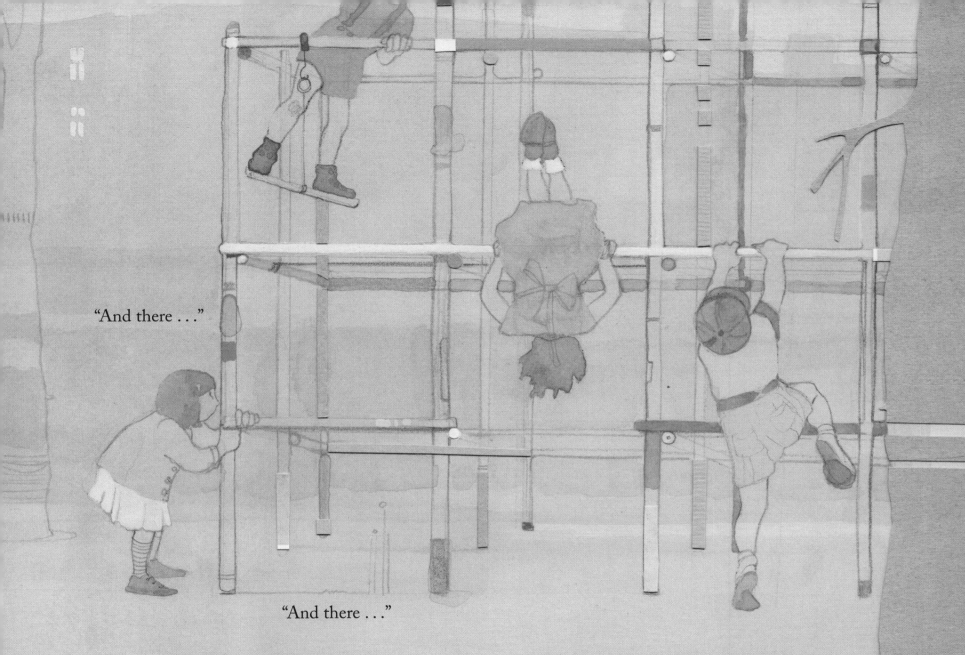

"And there . . ."

"And there . . ."

"Something real is felt here," he said,
putting his hand on his heart. "So the thing
you love can appear everywhere."

$\varphi = \bullet$

$\sqrt{4 + 3 + 6}$

In school Agnes learned about fractions
and the solar system.
    She liked to make equations and to think
about the moon.

Then one day, when she came home, everything was different.

Agnes became so sad that she stayed in bed.
She would not go to school.
She would not eat dinner.
She would not talk to anyone.
She could not find joy.

But many days later, she heard a voice in her mind.
She hurried to the park.

She saw it in a different way.
She got that feeling of the rainbow.
Here . . .

And there . . .

And everywhere . . .

She ran home and painted this . . . and that . . . and everything,
until she painted what was on the inside walls of her mind.

It was the feeling of beauty, and beauty became
the mystery she traced her whole life.

AUTHOR'S NOTE

Agnes Martin was one of the most esteemed abstract painters of the twentieth century. She created work that is revered all around the world, placing her in the company of painters such as Jackson Pollock and Mark Rothko.

Agnes was born in Saskatchewan in 1912 and died in New Mexico in 2004. She had a childhood on the prairies and later moved to Vancouver, New York and eventually to Taos.

In developing my story, I imagined that Agnes's sense of beauty was stirred by the mysteries of life and death in nature that she would have observed in her early life.

In her childhood and adolescence, Agnes spent considerable time with her grandfather, with whom she said she "felt first."[1] I wanted to explore how a special relationship like this might influence a burgeoning artist, and how abstract art could be seen as an expression of a feeling rather than an object. Abstract art is often seen to stand for virtues such as order, purity, simplicity and spirituality. I wanted to explore how Agnes's early sense of abstraction might have been formed by loss.

Agnes once watched a young girl staring at a rose. She asked the girl if she thought the rose was beautiful, to which the girl said yes. Then Agnes took the rose and hid it behind her back. "Is it still beautiful?" she asked the girl. The girl agreed that it was, and Agnes told her that was because beauty exists in the mind.[2]

I adapted this anecdote in order to give the mystery to Agnes as a young girl, implying that it might have been a revelation handed down to her by her grandfather, which she would eventually hand down to another young girl. The question for my fictional Agnes became "Where do things go when they disappear?" Agnes Martin's answer as an artist is that things stay in the mind and are deeply felt by artists who go on to express beauty in art. She said:

All art work is about beauty; all positive work represents it and celebrates it. All negative art protests the lack of beauty in our lives.

When a beautiful rose dies beauty does not die because it is not really in the rose. Beauty is an awareness in the mind.[3]

In real life, Agnes's grandfather died much later on, but in my story, Agnes's grandfather is like the rose. He will always be wherever she is aware of him in her mind.

1. Nancy Princenthal, *Agnes Martin: Her Life and Art* (New York: Thames and Hudson, 2015), 24.

2. "Arne Glimcher talks Agnes Martin at the Tate," Phaidon.com (2015): http://uk.phaidon.com/agenda/art/articles/2015/june/02/arne-glimcher-talks-agnes-martin-at-the-tate/.

3. Agnes Martin, "Beauty Is the Mystery of Life," in *Agnes Martin*, ed. Tiffany Bell and Frances Morris (New York: Artbook Monograph, 2015).